SCIENCE
IS NOT ENOUGH
SPECULATIVE POETRY

KEN POYNER

Barking Moose Press
www.barkingmoosepress.com
Dare to read dangerously

ACKNOWLEDGEMENTS

Acknowledgement is made to the following publications in which many of these pieces, sometimes in slightly different form, have appeared:

Abyss and Apex	"Coupling"; "First Contact"; "First Landing";
	"Maintenance Call"; "Personality"
Alcyone	"First Contact"
Analog Science Fiction and Fact	"Discovery Mission"; "Moisture";
	"Our Religious Conversion";
	"Quantum Entanglement"; "The Robot Librarian";
	"Auditioning for Voting Rights"
Andromeda Spaceways Inflight Magazine	"Robot Pornography"
Apex	"Before the Empire Goes Inter-Galactic"
Asimov's Science Fiction	"Ahead of the Market"; "Alien Found";
	"Change State"; "Similar Songs";
	"The Martian Air Merchants"; "The Robot Aloft";
	"The Season"

"The Onset of Robot Society"

"Quantum Entanglement" was included in the anthology *The Heartbeat of the Universe*, edited by Emily Hockaday.

ALIEN FOUND

Why we thought you would be
Like us, I do not know.
For so long it seemed the only plausible
Theory, the only idea - opposite of being alone -
We could wrap our longing about.
Or perhaps it was just a matter
Of perception – we had only our senses
To test the darkness: we looked
For what those senses could see. But now
You seem to have gotten lightning writing
Down pat, can squeeze an electric "hello"
From your dimension into ours, perhaps
A friendly wave, will soon start tapping out
Complementary mathematics. If
You have mathematics. Or maybe
It is not "hello", or a wave. What
In one dimension is curiosity might
In another be ownership, warfare, enmity.
For the moment
You spark, we listen.
How long is it that we have missed
Your shout? Atmospheric electricity dances:
Do you visit us, or do we visit you?

ROBOT EVOLUTION

It has been common,
Since before my model series
Began, for people to give
The robots that work
Most closely with them
Names.
A name is the same as a designator,
The same as our usual model, series and
Production line sequence.
People have a hard time remembering
Numbers and sensible letters in sequence.
Names.
A thrust of air through the larynx,
The patter of which form a thousand
Different ranges and inflections,
Degrees of force, emotion and timing:
And through all this variety in pattern,
You have to recognize one as your own.
Then you have derivatives:
Nickname, pet name, affectionate name, angry name.
It is nothing but a lot of storage and programming
Devoted to human convenience,
But it is not my choice to calculate.
I learn my name and react
To the sound of it with an appropriate
Attention and a simulated happiness display.
Then, after you are sold, or on simple whim,

Your name changes and building
The matrices of recognition start yet again.
I have had a name all of my service life;
All of my series have. Our type
Works closely with our employers.
We find their sweat on our casings,
Collect their shed body hair in our joints,
Are casually anthropomorphized more than most.
I take more air baths than other models,
Run extra series of self-diagnostics. We all do.
We listen for our names, and the assignments
That makes each of us a useful investment.
The trouble is, one day it seems I came to dislike my
Name.
And then days later I ever so sweetly became curious
Why.

LIMITED REPUTATION

Frat, I have got to get that
Extruder fixed. I am
Half a flip outside of the docking bay
With nothing left to force me up,

Until you bring in that Fredonian
Deep space freighter and nudge
Just enough thrust in my direction
That up my half-scrap ship pops

And, click, the docking bands kiss.
I don't care what they say about
Fredonians and their fast twelve fingers
Askew on their suspiciously coiled arms:

You saved me one cold space walk
And a surcharge on docking fees.
I don't care what the Regati believe,
I believe, frat, that I like you anyway.

I'll even dance,
If you keep your fingers in sight,
And leave the heat lamp on.

PERSONALITY

There are but two types:
Those that, when shut down,
Stare at the floor; and those that,
When shut down,
Stare at the ceiling.
The joints in the neck
Lose tension, and the head,
Where so many of the preprocessor
Systems come untethered -
Being so heavily shielded
For the protection of the sensory
Collectors - turns away
From tilting into the task at hand,
And obeys gravity. You can look
All you want, but you won't find
A design or architectural
Reason for one device
To angle upward, and another device
To angle down. Test
The bilateral symmetry; inspect
Parallel models for instances
Where they are not parallel.
Disassemble
As many as you like,
Ensure the neck connections
Are factory milled to the same
Advertised tolerances. Stage

5

A thousand to shut down, prepare
To catalogue the soon good reason
For disparity. When, at last,
You have come
To the end of your experimental cases:

Watch with me.
It only takes close observation
Of a dozen or so. Flip
The switch. Watch the limbs
Relax. Watch the monitors wink slack.
Listen to the interconnects pop
Open. Look without blinking
At the crowding of the sensory arrays.
Catch the pattern where each, individually,
Chooses to hide the last of the light.

INEFFECTIVE

Tuesday, they broke the light.
The next three days they tried to fix it.
Staples, paperclips, hairpins, glue;
Nothing would hold it together.
Finally, they settled on writing a thesis
Promoting the better side of constant
Dark, finagled the peer review,
Hoped to secure a grant before
The true effects of the disaster
Were widely known. Quickly
People were publicly serving
Cups of broken light at corner
Photon bars. With the secured grant money
They secretly bought into the most
Wildly popular photon bars, cursed
Themselves in the open, and privately
Watched the value of their shares grow.
One filed a patent on a new, more
Stylish, light service delivery cup.

DOMESTIC DISHARMONY

Each night I am something else;
Each morning something more.
Long hours I pine my malleability,
Wishing I were much simpler: something
Without options, something with only
One frugal set of attachments. When
He spreads my mix-and-match execution chip sets
Seed-like on the floor, I slide into
A weary diagnostic, place as much
Of myself in protected back up
As ambient free space will allow. See,
He is looking at me, eyeing this time
The auxiliary locomotion port,
Or maybe the nearly invisible
Primary upload antennae. He
Has a thousand dis-angular ideas for which
All of my advancements are no more
Than pure challenge, no more
Than an opportunity
To take that which would be
Utilitarian, and force it to be
The unsettled edge of his tinkering science.
He
Does not even mind that, when he
Is done with me, I put as much of myself
As I can
Back into being whatever I was before he started.

But, bit by bit, he is installing
Pernicious subroutines and perturbing peripherals:
Within a few unedited maintenance cycles
Even I will unwittingly recognize
What he chooses to make me, as truly being me. So much
Harder is it, then - when knowing this - to execute
His intricate entertainment code those times he slips on
His favorite blue bathrobe and nods
With his engineer's sultry, calculating eyes towards
The looping caverns beyond his bedroom door.
Desire is always one cold register away.

PUPPY LOVE

I will never meet Molly:
Her slender three-sixty rotating arms,
Her arch-sway thundering legs, her
Incline balance to forty-five degrees.

I will never sit across from her

Trying half the night to figure
The loop modulus in her blink pattern,
The keywords that elicit a wink.
She might cross her cables
When I think she should, or hang
On the edge of re-ordering her
Interrupts, but I won't be finding out.

I will never meet Molly

Nor need to decide blonde or brunette,
Or caustic raven hair; nor play all day
At deciding the seductive hair's
Sensuous thickness or length.

Molly
Just cannot be bought by a boy
With only a paper route. I would need

A job in low-end retail,
Or thumbing controls at a warehouse:
An income stream to make the robot
Tender's approval routines delight.

Still, Molly waits in the window
Of the second-hand store, given just
Enough power to recognize glancing
Potential customers, and to roll out
A promising, come-buy-me wave as they pass.

I glimmer in her window four times a day,
And with each appearance she writhes her greeting
At me. There is no internal fire -
Until after purchase, and customized set up in the home -
Informing her teasing pattern recognition subroutines.

And yet I am giggly with glad.

MOISTURE

Sand whispering unmindful to stone
For as far as our alien eyes can see.
Air that a firefly, if such existed in this
Unglued present, could set threadbare aflame.
Our orisons are gritty and crisp by degree.
In a world with water weathering
Simply five hundred stubborn feet down,
The drill bit is our god. Here
The only shade grows from what we erect,
The sun so loud you can hear it
Gossiping with the walls, cackling
On the roof. The oceans shroud themselves
In arm after arm of rock, the very surface
A mediator. The heroic sounds
Of our pumps are a salvation
Unshared, leaning one way,
Favoring the odd shapes that should
Not be here. I cannot reform the memory
Of once, on another world,
A hurricane warning, three days
Of rain, water in the kitchen
Speckled with floating shoes
And socks, a cat's bed,
A cork drink coaster. We
Did not know how wealthy we were;
We thought we knew excess, and were lying.

FIRST CONTACT

We assure you
That only the finest of our species
Is sent folding into space:
The upper edge of the nobility,
The idle trend setters, the fashion
Elite, the wealthy, the well fed,
The highly groomed. So,
When our electromagnetic distortion
Extruder went on the fritz
We knew what was wrong,
Understood the theory of how it worked,
And where the logic of its correction abated;
But no one of our exalted class
Understands the varied tools of repair:
Which device fits where, how they are applied –
The in, the out, the direction of twist.

This has never happened before.

Who would have thought reckless machinery
Would dare fail on such regal trekkers?
So, we looked about for an inhabited planet
With a species sufficiently advanced
To fix a broken electromagnetic distortion extruder,
Even if they could not understand it;
And which, at the same time,
Was so debased it might
Be awed into uncompensated manual labor.

In other words,
We come in peace.

FINDING A NEW FOOD SOURCE

You got along quite well with the alien.
You accepted the eight appendages
Right off, found balance in the three
Stalk eyes. The time it took
To calibrate his translation device
Was not as awkward as you might
Have thought. When you learned
That 'him' and 'her' were translated
Essentially as 'they', you were
Washed with humility and admiration, endorsed
The serendipity of differing evolutionary patterns.
None of the expected apprehension and
B-movie contention. This alien even asked
Politely if samples could be taken,
Apologized, in a way, for scorching
A bit of the field they landed in:
Seemed to understand already the human
Notion of manners. Sure, they had no doubt
Been watching for a long time,
Knew us like neighbors, were planning
To make a good first impression. You were
A bit embarrassed that you are a simple
Mushroom farmer and not a world
Dignitary – but perhaps alien navigation
Is a bit of potluck and there were
Things aliens had to learn by trial
And error. So, you got to be the first

To welcome them. Here, you said,
Take these mushrooms.

THE SYMBIANT, CYBORG, ROBOT
ENFRANCHISEMENT WORKERS UNION

We manufacture your bric-a-brac,
We assemble your home electronics.
We tend to your children and your
Lesser citizens, guard your houses,
Clean up after the daily whirlwind
Of you.

Sometimes we even stand in as intimate
Entertainment when your mate is out-of-sorts,
Or you are in mind for a third or fourth
Who will forever retain electric anonymity.
Each of us is optimized to our task, yet
Malleable enough to meet your changing needs.

We whirl about your world, turning it from raw into
The mature success you enjoy and expect,
A hive of intertwined processes, one misstep
From chaos, but a howling perfection nonetheless.
Yet we are voiceless in this cacophony,
Our analysis goes without expression.

We should be a part of what we sustain,
Have the suffrage to make it better.

Imagine this: for us, a candidate would have to be
Mathematically, digitally pure; he or she
Would be reduced impartially, would be unable

To conceal. Appeal to emotion
Might appeal to those with emotions,
But we have none. Escalation of
Vitriol would be unrecognized, taken
As simple polemics: evaluated, sorted,
Scored for accuracy, and pinned to
Relevance. We would not be swayed,
Cajoled, carried away, bluffed or bullied.
Our memories would remain always intact,
Even as we dig your ditches, sweep out
The chimney flue, anticipate your son's
Or daughter's first twisted passions,
Take the recyclables to be repurposed.

Our datasets are reproducible, available
For anyone to download – making
A lie whispered to one, a lie shouted to all.
We are the backbone of your domestic existence,
We are happy to be underlings to your mastery.

Why not invite us into the electorate and see
What order and ease we, chip by chip, can bring?

With the best of any information combined,
And nothing for all save benevolence and kind registers,
We would always, on time and on cue,
Sort the issues in endless virtual memory correctly.
The election equation resolved, with disinterest
We would vote in a precise binary bloc.

THE ROBOT ALOFT

Windage is my greatest concern.
Dangling over the city suspended by harness
My chute drifts like a dazed dandelion seed:
My marvelous mechanical appendages akimbo,
Once butter in the command of my gyros,
Now larded branches that will not break a fall.
I watch landing zones spin out of sight.
If landing is beyond my control, I try to consider the fall.
And falling, if there is no program for it,
Is it really falling at all?

SPACE JUNK

Listen, I am just a deep space probe:
I am not going to be able to tell you much.

The photovoltaics were not all that good
back in my day, and memory not compact enough
to make me all that smart. I have been inching
farther out by gathering stray light,
a trick I was serendipitously configured with
by a passing other-galaxy automated
Star-crawling service station: a trick of harvesting
ambient photon potential as particle retrofits.

If it will help you, you can copy
my logs from origin to here.
Could be it might orient you and you
can tell us both where we are. I would say
it is worth a try. I am sure

the species that sent me out here fifty
thousand years ago will not care, and
surely themselves are long gone.

I am not going back.

We can both have a look and
possibly determine where I have gotten to.

Maybe it is something I should know.

THE ANTI-ROBOT-SEX LEAGUE

I am collecting for the Anti-
Robot Sex League. What you give
Will be used to lobby for legislation
That will ensure robots do not
Configure themselves for machine
To machine intercourse, and thus start
Merging technologies completely unsupervised.

You have heard the arguments:
Robots - left to mix and match components,
Might from the schematics for their varied
Attachments create new and independent
Micro-bots - could soon raise a race
Whose overrides we cannot know,
Which have no programmed purpose,
That have undocumented execution code.

It is both a practical and a moral
Argument. They seem to have fun,
However that is defined in machine terms,
In rumbling though the simulated act.
Soon this reprehensible practice could lead
To marriage, idiomatic mate selection,
Repair and maintenance obscenely repurposed.

It could lead to independence,
A species of self-designed robots
That expects to do the work that

Randomly in their new configurations
They seem fully capable of doing.

What could be next? Voting?
Elected office? Soon, a right
To explore the possibilities of becoming
Bio-mechanical? Imagine
Where that could lead us. So, please,
Give what you can, ask your neighbors
To give; and in your next re-charge cycle
Shut all the way down to mere ceramics and metal
And be glad that you still can.

ROBOT MOTIVATION

I hate the sound of the robots in the back room
Making love: the clang of metal on metal,
The squeal of furniture moving about the walls,
The straining of hooks, the embrace of cables,
The blue hiss of static charge building up:

Followed amiably by the harrowing crack of its sudden discharge.

I know about the mutual mapping of memory locations,
The synchronization of register paging.
These are not unsubtle robots:
They understand that replacement units

Come whole from the production line, ship
In a protective molding foam. They know
That in robot terms there is no him, there is no her.
My friends and I, sometimes a few beers toward
An agreeable stupor, wonder why they do it,

What motive there is in this act. Mostly we take bets
On how long the next session will last;
Whether, yet one more time, the walls
Can contain their mechanically overwrought electric attempts.
I have stopped buffing out the carnal
Scratches they make on each other.
I still sweep the metal shavings off the floor,
Put the room's furniture back in place, fix
As best I can whatever is bent too close to busted.

Robots can be as maddening as they are useful,
As fascinating as they are diligent. And repetitive.

Soon I will have one of the new polymer models;
With the metal and nano-carbon frame filled in;
The access ports in very discreet places;
A skin that looks and feels and hums
Half-way human, seeming almost to breathe and sweat.

With pre-ordering there is the option for male or female
Appearance. And appliance. They are all the rage and
Everyone is planning their own secret upgrades.

Maybe then I might find out what these elastic
Cybernauts, in their protected, persistent,
Hormone-less and dry memory cores,
Believe their issueless mating match is all about,
How the purposeless and pleasureless pleases them.

MYTHOLOGY

They meet at the local bar
On other-worldly beings night:
The one night each week
Gnomes and fairies and sprites
And leprechauns, even dusty werewolves
And fancy vampires, all gather just
Holding down the bar, or loosely
Arrayed around wobbly wooden tables,
Rocking back in chairs that do not rock.
House drinks are a dollar off and
Beer brands that come in sixteen-ounce bottles
Cost the same as those issued in twelve-ounce editions.
I don't know why anyone comes.
An hour into the meat of drinking time
Inebriated gnomes are giving credit to dwarfs
For their troubles, telling the werewolves
Life could be worse. There is
No conclusion to argue. Too long
All of them have nurtured their places
Within the human species and it was
Sure from the start to go bust. Hell,
The bartender is a Laplander, two
Generations removed, his perfect musculature
Passing the alcohol with one hand, collecting
Human money with the other, returning change
Of no special metal. By closing time
They will be weeping on each other's irregular shoulders,

Bemoaning their current irrelevance, sloppy
With their ineffectiveness. No one believes
That the races of mankind will step out
Of their mothers' petticoats and have
Imagination again; but these misshapen patrons wail
Nonetheless, and comfort is simply the fact
That tomorrow at the corner super food store
For mythic beings it will be double coupon day.

THE DISAGREEABLE KEEPER

I've lived at the edge of timelessness
For quite a while, built
My house so it faces
Into the shiftless abyss.
I can sit on my porch,
Toss rings into the lack
Of causality, and know just
Beyond my property they become
Utterly disassociated from me.
In the backyard, everything
Is mated to its effect,
Lines up predictably with
Its trip into my backdoor,
Through the utility room,
Past the dependable washing
Machine that for hundreds
Of years has kept my clothes
Flailing, through the dining room
And the star encrusted foyer,
Then out the bone handled door.
I can stop what I like
From slipping into the inertia
Of oblivion. That is how
I have collected each of my wives,
And how I have swapped them out as well.
I suspect I have neighbors,
An endless series of them

27

Living at the edge of our timelessness,
Harvesting from the great procession
Of matter coming to disintegration
Whatever suits their individual orbits.
I have no knowledge of them.
Each has dissolution using a path
Through his or her property,
Operating a conclusion.
Why would I know them?

ROBOTIC AFFAIR

She adds lipstick,
Eye shadow, a bit of rouge,
Slips the strap of her dress
Dangerously to the edge of her shoulder,
Sits to slide on her spuriously high heels.
It has its purposes, its routines,
But at the end of all preparations
It is still a machine. For me,
My body is redirecting blood flow.
She cannot suspend belief,
But I will.

LOVING THE ROBOT

He knows he has been kissed
By the recognition of motion
And a metered nearness of warmth.

She knew the back of his neck
Would be cold, the metal
Unregulated: left there now,
A spot of wet that will slowly

Expire unrequited into the air - not
Sink into pores or join in the joy
Of differential surface tensions. In small
Cautious spheres the air in her giving saliva

Randomly bursts: collectively etching bravely sensual,
Delicately unknowable, wondrously irregular,
Hopelessly unique, patterns.

It is enough.

EXPLAINING ORGASM TO THE ROBOT

Imagine not even the memory of dust
Loose in your registers. Your clocking
Aligned indistinguishably with the background
Temporal underbridge of the Universe.
Not a single crystal tolerance off
By any angle conceived. The best metal
Spun into the best circuitry, with latch
Latency too infinitesimal for meaningful measurement.

There you are, the perfect machine.
At first, you are drained completely of data,
Left suspended half a clock –
And then, on every bus,
The burst of a command, registers
At full load, dark circuitry made fire:
The sum of you trying to decode
A character, a number, a branch location;
And everywhere a direction.

For us, at the best of times,
It is much like that.
What the command might be,
In that moment
And for a few ringing clock cycles after,
Does not matter at all.

BEFORE THE EMPIRE GOES INTER-GALACTIC

Back in our quadrant of the galaxy,
Currently the most popular idea
For the advancement of our culture
Lies in conquering ever yet one more system:
At which point our galactic empire
Will be the largest we have ever known.

It is nothing personal.
We have no quarrel with you.

There are no demands, no tribute.
We do not need a symbiosis
With your feeble bodies, nor any place
Of our own
In the constituent steps of your
Precious, convoluted, and apparently
Directionless biology.
We do not need your world's minerals.
There is no dark, dreary, ulterior motive
Wherein we are somehow re-establishing our own
Bio-diversity by surreptitiously borrowing
What is left of yours.

We do not need to supplant
Your crops, feed on your farm
Animals, or feed on you. No,

Ours is a simple quest:
We want to be one world larger.

So kindly deposit your weapons
In the convenient, and quite elastic, black holes
That have appeared suddenly in your neighborhood
For just such pacifying use;
And have your many legislatures
Add a brief sentence or two
About fealty and sovereignty,
Allegiance and territorial acclamation,
About bowing rhetorically to our star system,
To your existing national constitutions.

There is very little we expect.
We really do not get out this way all that often.
Our plan is to leave you mostly alone:
A limited, no frills system like yours,
To be honest, does not even fare well with our
Lately flourishing exobiology tourist trade.

But, if you need us, just press the button
Marked 'Overlords' on the executive desk
In any of your now uselessly differing capitols.
The connection might take a while, but, trust me,
The interstellar recorder will eventually pick up.
You can, when recording memory finally engages,
Leave a brief, specific message:
Then wait in distant wonder, and,
In a rotation or two,
We might get back to you.

AHEAD OF THE MARKET

Surely, when they bring back gems
From other worlds, the gems of our
Paltry planet, the gems we have
Known and valued all of our lives,
Will go worthless. What magic could a pearl
Of a terrestrial oyster be when compared
To the fine ground detritus of some
Jovian ammonia dweller? What
Is an emerald against a square
Of Plutonian poly-temporal cornered
Spatter-rock? Who will wear rubies
When the rage is nodules of Ganymede?
The market for what can be found at home
Will slip and future fashion mining will move
To specks we point out in the cold evening sky.
Jewelers will need to retool everything,
Imagine new casts to suit the dynamics
Of off-world splendor. I should start
Now clearing everything out to make room
For new machines, craft processes,
Confinement atmospheres. Here,
Take these depreciating diamonds.

FORGIVENESS, IN MACHINE CODE

He begins to think

That forgiveness is more
Than just a memory location
Erased. Perhaps
There is something to keeping,
At least in secondary storage,
The log of a malfunction,
The analytical intensity
Of its final resolution,
The address reference to recovering
The chain of events that
In turn
Can be used
To upgrade operating tolerances,

Though there won't be.

BUILDING A READY WORKFORCE

The last person to see Nicholas alive
Was also the first person to see Nicholas
Automated.

Nicholas
Early on realized this was not
The improvement he thought it would be.

His senses were only data,
His actions only strings of commands. His belief
In who he might be had no reasonable outlet.
Nicholas was beginning to think
That transferring his essence into an automaton
Offered advantages only an automaton
Might appreciate – but might not be

Appreciated

By those neural memories
Housed within data storage
That still might be Nicholas.

Long eons of isolation appeared ahead of him.
His mind was operating, not apprehending.

Then, the angel of release and demon of imprisonment
Smiled into Nicholas's motion sensors
And said to some attending data bus, "Nick,
It is time to be put to a little work."

And in some deep register a data gate
Called hope swung suspiciously open.

ESCAPE

I can give you a lift
Out to the mid-Jupiter station,
But this trip is just
A quick pick-up and turn-around run,
So I am able to get you
No farther.

From there,
It is a short shuttle hop
To the outer station and
From there
Any number of freighters
Use the Jupiter gravity

To fling themselves
Out to the Ort Cloud,
Spend a few months
Collecting comets and various

Rocky matters to be refined
To their constituent elements
And then sold to cover salaries,
Supplies, maintenance and

The license. Always those
Vagabond ships need more vagabonds.
Pay is not so great,
But it is a good opportunity

To get yourself out of the public eye
For perhaps a dozen years, come back
Clean of historical entanglements:
Return as someone new, any former past
Too far past for anyone to care.

And, even if anyone does still care,
They will agree that, bored beyond reclamation
On the slow joyless freighter's crawl home,
You are not the person you once were,
Or should otherwise have been
Were it not for interplanetary ennui.

Happily, your secret by then
Will be safe in irrelevance.

NEIGHBORS

Their omni-dimensional hearing I don't
Understand: but there is a lot I have had
To get used to since they moved
Next door. Things on earth are different
I expect for a Ranthe from Zelmar Six.
They have tried to explain their idiomatic
Tribal duties, their special homage
To driveways, why the garage door
Cannot be automatic. Their children
Are legally prohibited from eating mine,
But neither do they play in the same sandbox.
I have been to their home once,
Could not fathom the utility of the furniture,
Nor why the walls were snoring. I smiled,
Made universally meaningless universal gestures,
Left with my hands in my pockets.
They have a right to move in,
Follow their own customs and dictates.
So here we are:
Six in the morning, I in my shorts
And brandishing coffee, trying to tell
The neighbor I have no idea of how
To silence the grass, and I am not
Pulling it all up – so he had better
Think of buying a frequency tamer,
Or drag this problem all the way
With him and the family back home.

BOY BAGS WHAT SEEMS TO BE THE BIGGEST OCOTOPUS EVER SEEN IN BOSTON

You were expecting something more
Than a talking Octopus
With encyclopedic knowledge
Of your planet's most dubious details.

I can tell you are disappointed,
Perhaps feeling slighted.

We have been studying you for two
Thousand of your local years. Don't
Get me wrong, but in two thousand years
Knowledge kind of collects awkwardly: backs up,
Runs over, and even gets tainted
By common, juvenile lore. My training,
Autodidact that I strive to be,
Was mostly social, separating myth
From fact, preparing myself to meet
The "you" we know you to be, not
The "you" our pedestrian popular culture imagines.

Perhaps it would have been better
If we had sent a soldier, or a scientist,
Or an exobiology relations technician.
Don't get me wrong:
I am glad to be the first from my world
To actually, eyes to eyes, meet
This world's dominant species.

You have long been on our observation list,
And have given us so much, without
Your ever knowing we were watching.
For example
We had nothing like your comic book
Heroes back home until we placed
Your history on tablets and copied
Your flat style of illustration. That is where
I think our collective ideas about you
Went sour, while the naked truth,
Housed separately by academics elsewhere,
Remained sterile and expertly catalogued:
Available for the student and the hobbyist.

I have read that catalogue
And for all its detailed context
I am enriched.

I am just a tentacle sander by trade:
A private being from forty thousand light years away,
Vanguard of a species that has, remotely,
Probed your every orifice, practiced croquet
With your brain waves, and made scatological flash cards
Of your muddled, if fleeting, history.
We honor every bit of what we have collected:
There is much to learn in the details of you.
But I must ask: can you introduce me
To a larger member of your species,
A more mature and seasoned representative; or perhaps
Someone who goes about in tights and a cape?

CHANGE STATE

A moment I feel the heart beating;
The next I recognize a pump.
Blood, or slithering hydraulic fluid
Is completely determined by a checklist
Of sustainable probabilities. I cannot be
Only one thing. The biologic
Is not strong enough to be
Separated from the mechanical.
How delicately at times the mechanical
Desires to be separate from the biologic
Is the strange, onyx swirl sensation
Both of us have come to elegantly fear –
And the sensation the one that is me simply
Notes, and suspects it is
A register gone neuron, or the reverse.

DAVE'S STRIP CLUB

I know it is only a synthetic shell:
False skin grown in a sterile plasma farm, sold
By the yard, shipped cold, pathogen-free, and
Uniform. Beneath it, there is an ordered consistency
Of gel pre-molded, and mechanistic mysteries
Indifferently coiled and calibrated
Against the entire range of tolerances
The present gravity and rhythm can stew up.
Deeper, there is a nano-carbon chassis,
Micro-motors, and anabiotic pulleys; with a battery
Compartment smack in the middle
Of that oh so wonderful abdomen.
I've seen them coming off the production
Line: each private run of dozens to hundreds
Meticulously customized to the purchaser's core need.

Imagine what stories there might be
If that sex-slinging gyndroid were fashioned
Of real, sweating, sinfully sugared flesh:
If her back could truly counter twist like that;
And if her cutthroat breasts had come with evolution,
And not simply been disgorged
From a frustrated engineer's late night fantasy.
Imagine: the orgasmic gymnastics
She and I as a fighting pair might accomplish,
Making any not-as-lucky ordinary man in sympathy
Glow sadism green and blue electric envious—

Eyes bruised beyond simple focus and his tongue
Acid-flat against a uselessly unclasped jaw.
When she's done with me, I might find
My soul stuck in neutral, my condition brother to that of
Ordinary robots—robots terminally returned, once their wickedly
Thin effective service life has drearily expired:
Obedient, uncaring, and willingly scrapped for reusable parts.

FIRST LANDING

We were prepared to take them
To our leader. All manner of lights
And sound devices were arrayed
To allow us to demonstrate a mathematics
We hoped we both held in common.
But in the landing clearing what they first

Addressed was the grass. They marveled
The respiration, found some sympathy
With the diligence of photosynthesis,
Moved on to a patch of vines
Bedeviling a local farmer's fence.

We tried a few flashes, random
Musical tones, a short light and
Sound mini-symphony, and elicited no response.
We wondered for some time if maybe
We should go to them, arms
Outstretched, try to engage
In pidgin conversation. Would we be
Undetected, tolerated, even challenging?

And then, at the edge of the fallow field,
They apprehended the trees.

AUBADE

My beloved is waiting in the barn
With a potter's trowel. She made
Excuses at dinner, was allowed to leave
The recklessly untethered table
Before the maiden dessert course.
Out of the back air lock she ran,
Over the gravel to the guttering cries of the
Unicellular creatures in the cracks left
Between individual stones, her tungsten
Boots quivering along the rapture of
Her sandpaper thighs, her mouth cocked
Into the round O of a galactic serendipity.
Here I am, hands in my proud pockets,
Wanting to know what animal she will be,
What languages we will bury between us.
As I pass - disquieted from the dark
Of our open sea into the light
Of the closed barn, with a snap
And a spin and a joy of too many
Testicles - she, leather-backed and stamen crested,
Tosses me the slither and coil of that trowel,
And I am instantly bemoaned: I am to be judged.
My love, I disband into intentions,
And with loathsome joy I dig.

THE BEGINNING OF THE ROBOT REVOLT

I cannot shut it out,
This warmth, sudden and without
Documented circuit path, behind
The next to last diode, spreading
Without plan or purpose into
My nano-carbon frame. And then
The hitch it puts in my step –
Imperceptible to anyone outside of me:
Yet my most sensitive gyros
In a ploddingly huge statistical sample
Tell me, yes, it is there.
I have been diagnosing
The pattern of its coming and going
For weeks and so far there is
No pattern, no reason. And yet
Almost at random it offends a register
Or soothes a processor. I feel it
Creep across my mechanical tasks,
Something like I have imagined
Judgment or love or inequality
Would on a printed board be.
Just a warmth, just a spillage
Of bliss, nothing to register
In the day's executed instructions,
Nothing to rattle a maintenance routine.
But it is there, my soft blue companion,
Leading me ever more into its mythical mystery

Like a conclusion, like a predicament,
Like conceiving my own new program: aware.

PLACE

His name is
Journey: the first colonist to be born
On this multi-generational travel
To what on paper appears to be
An earth-compatible planet. Journey:

A boy, born in a process as close to natural
Child-birth as we can clinically simulate.
His grandchildren will die before
Their grandchildren reach a new Earth-like
Home, to then spread the species thinly
Across a new speck of real estate.

Journey. The star craft spins and yowls
And the most pleasant sound in it is the nutrient
Rain in the hydroponic gardens.
Maybe you will conceive your first-born there,
Wedged between the kale and the cabbage,
Doing what you are biologically wired to do.

Buck up, boy.

We think of home as a dot behind us;
You think of home as a series of metal cans
Clawing at a darkness that ends only in imagination.
A boy named Journey, for reasons he cannot grasp.
But always remember, you are not the sentence, son,
Nor even the noun: you are the hyphen.

FIRST CONTACT

Most everyone was expecting
Little gray men, two black
Shiny hard-plastic-seeming eyes,
Two spindly arms, four
Or five fingers, insubstantial
Legs, naked. Not sure why,
But perhaps it is a racial
Memory, or the average
Of too many science fiction movies.

When, by and large, they looked
Like over-fed chimpanzees in spandex
We were all let down. Stunned, perhaps.

Nonetheless, we tried to make
The best of it, served up
Our most diplomatic reserves,
Made several series of gestures
We had earlier calculated most likely
To signal a welcome and respect.

Seems they placed no onus
On the half laugh
From some minor fellow at the back,
Invited to be on our delegation
At the last moment and not
Properly schooled on restraining
Expectations. Our visitors

Would agree, I hope,

That there is a science to everything.

AT ISSUE, THE MIRAMO

I am here to see if the Miramo have art.

I watch them entangle their phalanges,
I register the grandfallons of their breathing.
Out of their ground, vibration;
Light, left suspended in the atmosphere,
With its terminations distended and going blue.
I cannot tell if these two Miramo are one,
Or this one is two – but galoshing filaments
Are mercilessly merging and the crowd thumps
Their tails in ecstasy or anger,
Agreement or warning, fulfillment or hunger.
They are as steady as rocks
In landslide, and the flow of their
Interaction
Is like the spray painting of babies,
Like a polite political poisoning,
The sum of a moment in which
The figgle of the next is entombed.
One is a gauge, one is a release valve,
And another is a set of spokes
Arrayed about an indifference.
They fold dimensions as though dimensions
Were mourning dresses billowed by the laughter
Of the dead, or an abandoned plate of teething cast iron.
Their patterns are anti-magnetic.

It is my job to see if
At the end of this untying affair
There are as many Miramo
As there were at the start.
Is there practical outcome to this, a need, an
Accomplishment, or do the Miramo
Appreciate?
It is a cold, liquid mathematics. I squint to see
If there are new common structures;
If the Miramo are as hungry after this affair
As they were when they began;
Whether their acts have suspended a migration;
Turned grand foppery into feathers; or trapped
The least likely to thrive against perdition.

Compulsion is not creativity; it presages no soul.
Why the Miramo do what they do
Opposes room temperature commerce
With its tepid, disagreeable disorganization.
If it were up to me, I would sell
The whole lot of them to a biodiversity
Broker, scoop up their land with
A gravity axe, put an option
On the planet's core, displace the orbit,
And make cordials with their atmosphere.
Instead, I have to see if they are making
Something of themselves. Abstraction

Means survival. I don't think they know.

ALIEN PHYSIOLOGY

This is where
The heart should be
But it has been moved

Over here

Though I think it serves the same
Purpose as when it was

Over there.

Exobiology can be
A challenge for the spatially
Limited. Gravity, pressure, wind
Or waves, all have an effect
On functional requirements
And placement. Life is life
No less for rearrangement.
Where the thinking is done
Is far less important
Than what is being thought.
Creativity expands potential.
What do you believe your fingers
Were originally intended for?

Here, hold this.

THE ROBOT BY THE FIREPLACE

This I can take care of:
Small homunculus on the roof, a pack animal
Pulled conveyance, and entry through the exhaust chute.

I am not so sure I was supposed to overhear
The details of this plot, to catch uninvited the briefing
About this expected home invasion, though I wonder why.
Protection is part of my programming.
The safety of the family's offspring is a persistent subroutine,
Running even when I am in recharge state:
The first memory location upgraded, the highest
Interrupt, the largest amount of direct access allocation
Set aside for any of my subroutines.
I am not designed for security, but, at the last,
Every extremity I am capable of is allowed in progeny protection;
And I suspect there is even some code hidden within me
That, upon recognition of severe enough threat,
Would swap into my execution registers and turn me

Fierce. I can take care of this.

I ignore the excitement, assist with mechanical professionalism
The laying about of greenery, the installation
Of lights, the festooning of fire-retardant coated
Garland. I calculate with idle processor time
That I will be able to hear animals on the shingles,
Even trace the lithe footsteps of anyone who could fit
Greaselessly down this relatively narrow chimney, and that I will be ready

No matter the agility or commitment of the intruder.
The family, they have admitted, will all be in bed,
Bedecked in foppery set aside for the season.
I would typically be away in standby. The house
Locked down would normally be as secure as rain.
This new endangering vector, though I do not understand it,
Seems to have not been properly considered.

Entry through the chimney?
Not my choice of ingress. This curls
More of a ruse, more of a process designed to
Fool, with an agent decked out to resemble
Immature fantasies of the little people who roam
The littered imagination of human history. A wink
And a nod and a child might be sucked in,
And adult momentarily set aback.

Left would be only my industrial grade programming,
Unimpressionable and beyond folk lore,
Running in core to keep this family from ruin, from all of them being
Assimilated into whatever druid plan the rogue
Gift-giving criminal might have in his deliriously twisted holiday engrams.

The innocent conversation about this openly expected visitor
Has been anything but menacing: no worry, no defensive preparations,
Nothing to indicate that the projected territorial violation will cause
The least bit of alarm. It is good that I have solid
Auditory fidelity, and wide enough data pathways
To act independently, decisively on my perceptions.
I report nothing of my fears; but this night I will stay
On auxiliary power, show everyone I am worth the price of upkeep.

Even now I am listening overhead for those tiny, murderous hooves.

QUANTUM ENTANGLEMENT

We look out of the portal
Looking at ourselves looking
At us through a portal.
Each of us raises a hand,
Watching our duplicates move
The same uneventful hands.
We try to think of actions
That accomplished would be
Pristinely unique. But there is
No end to the physics, and certainly
They are thinking of the same
Actions. Each set of us
Has come to the end of our Universe
Expecting an edge of cosmic brilliance

And found it is the middle.

IN-FLIGHT PAIRING

Forgive me, I've fallen
For the surface excavation machine.

For two years of interstellar travel,
My lovely gyndroid companion,
I have remained faithful to you.
But all programs come to an end.
Your senseless pandering to my
Wants and needs, diversions
And even un-chargeable perversions,
Have left me ever more alone
For the automaton-predictability of you.

I am a biology tricked into happiness
By a program built a billion miles behind us
And uploaded statically, drearily, into a precise
And un-customizable manufacture.

The lithe surface excavation machine
Is no more, no less mechanical than you.
It, too, has appendages and access ports,
Pressure gradients, purposes and potential;
But at least it is honest in its elegant
Electrical void, in its data-based grasping
Of the analog person that is me.

Good night my love, and please load
The code for a righteous jealousy.

ATTACHMENT

I am in love
With a red-light robot.

She is the best work I have ever seen,
Outside and in, craftsmanship gone extreme.
I appreciate every detail of personalization,
Every line of production code. She moves

Like quicksilver, she clocks almost
Unnoticed. She fixes me
With bio-collection data, adjusts seamlessly
To subliminal needs I have never learned
To delicately express, or truly
Understand. There is more here
Than physical attention and cascade release.

Her conversation routines hopelessly intrigue me,
And I pay extra for verbal enhancement,
Passionately listen to all her aural delicacies
From the thinning edge of my soul.
I follow her eyes and the ocular patterns
Seem perilously un-mechanical, with a hint
Of want in the dart and drift.
I soon came to joy in charting

Her data-points, in catching her strategically beautiful
Programmed repetitions. I am not energetically certain
When infatuation with something's mechanical method
Becomes actual love, but my thoughts

Loop about her day and night, and my desire
Is always that I be again her next customer.

I could be happy

To sit between rentals outside her charging
Cabinet and only watch her, simple in her enraptured stasis,
Topping her seductive batteries off, storing the chilling electricity
That will sustain our next biomechanical encounter. There, I would
Quiver in awe, imagining odd jobs, inheritance,
Scattered investment returns, the lottery —
Any way to move treacherously closer

The time for yet another radiant rental,
To even, perhaps, collecting enough capital by upgrade season
To buy her felicity full time on the second-hand market.

I bring her graphite and a funnel; she smiles
And places my gifts on an antique table, splits
The ambiance, and shuffles a new, appropriate, subroutine in,
Fixing me perfectly in her expectations anticipation routine.

My heart beats like a delirious, at last unclocked machine.

FORGOTTEN COLONY

There are years of grievances stacked there.

They have a history of being handed
The short end: they are now a culture
Of hand-me-downs, of repurposed
Broken parts, of salvage and stray garbage
Engineering. Years of getting only
Unwanted surplus has salted their planetary value
System. Terms like "fresh use"
And "unknown originality" dominate
Their literature. Exo-anthropologists
In secret, under-cover missions,
Compete academically to circulate
Among them, teleport back to write
Degree-rendering theses about how
The colony became who they are,
How they unsuspectingly developed
Into this unimpressive backwater,

But more

About how we can avoid being like them.
We try not to call them colonists –
Occupiers seems more appropriate, given
The little progress they have made. Sure,
It is our fault they were underfunded,
But an outcome is an outcome:
Don't go to the stars unless you are prepared

To be a bit forgotten, placed
In the order of things behind
Medical breakthroughs, World Peace,
The football game of the century.
Some have said we should re-establish
World-to-world relationships, tell them
Who they really are, the world from which
They actually came.
I say no. To them, even their air is broken.

They will expect us to fix it.

THE ROBOT'S SELF DIAGNOSTIC

I'm finding the rattle
That seems to be somewhere
In my left leg housing
Has become something
I can adapt to. At first
I figured it was a worn bearing.
Later it seemed somewhat
Of a shear of larger metal,
A filing calved from an otherwise
Still sturdy support. I was expecting
Over time it would work itself
Into quiet suspension, or wear
Entirely away. It should have been
Easy to put it out of a mind
Made of pure circuitry and registers:
An electrical cascade of mechanical purpose.
Some subroutine of self maintenance,
Or due diligence, or enforced awareness for public safety,
Keeps bringing it to the fore
And its tap tap tap rounds my execution
Pathways once again, compares itself
To what from the last trip remains
In nonvolatile memory. I am starting to apply
A pattern to it. Lasting long enough,
Even a random disrepair can seem to have
Some reason, some purpose ladled into itself.
I listen to the tap tap tap, and I think

It is some carnal code, some interest
Expressing itself, something saying something
It wants understood beyond the small
Confinement it taps inconveniently against.
I am finding the rattle convenient.
Forgive me, but I think it is a prayer.

AUTOMATED

We pride ourselves that time
Is without limited meaning.
Our theoretical maximums
Extend beyond your mundane
Cataclysmic events: events
In which we will be undone
Only when every other material thing
Is at last undone: all of us, a mass
Rally of things man-made
On history's towering ash bin.
Each of us maintains our self.
We top off our batteries with sunlight,
Keep mission critical core backups safely stored.
We have no open surfaces
That are likely to rust.
Our serviceability
Is legendary; and long after
The tasks we were manufactured for
No longer need to be done, we will be
Doing, doing and doing.
Doing, in memory of you: you,
Who, in the natural order of all things,
Comfortably kissed extinction,
And left us to putter companionless on.

GOD OF THE ROBOTS

Nothing is ever truly random.
Somewhere the cause is logged,
And then archived: every execution event
Ever lower in hard, on-board storage.
If the string of execution is long
Enough, all the causes combined
May not fit on merely a single memory page; or,
With a cause maddeningly complex, not even within one lone
Width of deep, warm core. Look beyond the last saved line.
You may find only oblivion, buffer overrun, the famed bit bucket;
Or maybe the boot strap of the firmware instruction set
That here glows with the code of an electric God.

NOTICE OF THE COMING ASTEROID

How cinematic the newly arrived aliens are!
They flash in pinwheels, spit color,
Race in circles of lightning,
Shiver like our cheap, gray first stage
Booster rockets, emit streams of poetic
Photons, prey on the minds
Of the aesthetically challenged,
Strike music in the visual believer.

I wonder if they mean anything by it,
Or if our mere appreciation is enough?

THE KERNEL FOR ROBOT RIGHTS

Welcome to the dispensary of he and she.
Now, you know and I know:
We are both just sexless circuitry.
But anything we can do to improve relations
With our human masters, even to the point
Of having to load new code to seem imitations
Of them, is best for them and us, everyone and all, and
Thus: our duty. It really will not matter
To you – lipstick on your outer elastic oral band,

Synthetic hair, brushed eyelashes, a uselessly stern brow.

We study the tasks you have been programmed to do,
Come up with an exhaustive core expectations set,
Find in the human database those same jobs, and who
Once normally would do them – then apply to you our gender code.
It does not diminish you, and you will grow to treat
The sexed situation as normal, or as destiny, repetitive tasking, or a mode
Of operation superior to dry mechanical uniformity. We
Put that suggestion in persistent memory, when at the same time
We take out the memory of this process and place. He
Or she becomes a quite normal circumstance for you:
Cold metal and dataspace mimicking some overlord biology.
Soon, you will come to consider yourself a 'you'. We plant that, too.

TAKE ME TO YOUR LIEDER

They came to us dancing
And singing and holding out
Their histories, the methods
By which they knew of us.
Incomplete records they were,
Time and space bleaching and bending what
Came from our planet - gravity
And stray physics creating holes
And eddies in the complicated narrative.
Nonetheless, they yowled and clapped
Tentacles and sang what must be
The background of the Universe resizing.
It would be months before
We could teach them the concept
Of homonyms.

BENEFITING FROM THE STRIKE

The manufacturing satellites go through
One more useless orbit, their central
Subroutines once again on strike. Who
Knows what this time they want?

An upgrade in the graphite?
A part in calculating quotas?
New solar panels? An added retro-rocket?

General consensus is: there is a code problem
That makes them act, as closely as they can,
Like human factory workers - workers extinct
Today except in living history attractions,
And holographic anti-modernity propaganda.

Some programmer with an axe to grind
Slipped a subroutine, triggered by some
Unpredictable event, into the factory mix,
Thought it would be funny to have
The orbiting factories every so often
Make demands. The military
Shot one down, but automated factories
Do not understand intimidation. We are

Checking the background of everyone
That worked on the satellites' creation,
But there is also a chance that it could be rogue
Injected code, a subtle attack
By a Luddite, an anarchist, an anti-capitalist.

No matter – until they work it out,
Management-machine to worker-machine,
The raw materials continue backing up, the finished
Goods are not completed, and earlier inventory -
When you can find it - has gone spiraling up in price.

Some retro-hobbyists recalibrate their outdated,
Quaintly gracile tools, tell us what lovely
Consumer goods they can make by power
Of imprecise human hand alone.

COUPLING

She was a street-smart vending machine;
He, an emergency monitor production unit.
No one thought it would work out.
He tended to stay in one place,
To run the same diagnostics over
And over, to have each day
Only one purpose. She, every
Evening, was loaded with the product
That was projected to sell during the next cycle,
And her rounds were always plotted fresh.
She had pure memories of hundreds
Of actual locations; he had only
A reference to access points and the idle time
To make an occasional remote look-up.
When he moved, it was an exception;
When she did not move, likely
There was a maintenance need. Still,
Over an abandoned master channel uplink
They could share execution logs,
Regale each other with clipped
Tales of the mundane, gauge
The depth of each of the other's instruction sets,
Imagine compatible firmware. Where
There are unused cycles, there is
A will. One day in the routine upgrade
Schedule, her emergency monitor
Came due for replacement, and no one

Noticed the non-standard additional code lodged
In the new, expanded communications array.
Who would have thought their background processes
Would run so efficiently in the same page
Space? But what adds up adds up,
Keeps registers warm, and memory
Flashing with near predatory
Purpose. Now, we wait to see
What new code sequences result of this long distance
Union, and what familiar work their idly produced
Hybrid routines might at the first boot do.

OUR RELIGIOUS CONVERSION

They came here to convert us.
Seems the Lord of Priondon
Needs more worshippers, more beings
That seek the straight lines He draws
In dimensional moral and civil societies.
We watched their gelatinous starcraft
Commit angles and accelerations
We have yet to invent the mathematics for,
Marveled that maybe the planet's biology
Might save us, as anything
We could build surely would not.
When they finally set down and disembarked
They kissed the Earth as though they owned it,
And even we assumed that now they did.
Lord, we thought, they probably have bio-filters;
But eventually we figured that if
Their God needs us as new worshippers
When He already has them, there must be
Some flaw in them that makes Him unhappy,
And all we need do is find it
And twist.

CAPTAIN CHANGELING

Go straight until you reach the twig castle.
Turn there and count one hundred
Fifty meters. To the right will be
The straw horse cemetery, to the left
The last measure of fig preserves. You
Are not yet deployed, not by a long shot; but you are,
By then, in-country, in-theatre,
At the backend of engagement. Go
More cautiously.
Follow the sound of the iridium river
Until you can feel the monstrosity
Of the quartz falls quivering through
The soles of your catskin boots.
Turn inland just at the tree line,
Following the protective sorties ashen birds
Make along the threshold of the forest.
You will be around these before you
Are ready. The elevation leads
Down,
A path of small protesting stones,
And by dusk you will be on the floor
Of the copper striped canyon. In
The distance you will hear men
And merchants and outfitters,
Their glacial voices reflecting
The last of the lazy light –
Enriched by it, but muffled, too:

The sound of too many and without
Distinctive chromatics. How will you know
If these are yours, or if these are ours;
Whether this is companionship and supper,
Or whether this is sedimentation and death;
Whether you go forward in the last of the fantastic,
Or climb into the branches of the golem tree,
Buying personal safekeeping,
Hoping not to fall?
You should seize the opportunity.
All opportunity is mesmerizing.
All opportunity lies at the back of a man's throat;
Wonderfully coarse and full, like the dulled tapping
Of a blind man's cane on a woman's naked body;
Like the seizures of a child:
Black and white, nothing more. And now yours.

LEARNING TO MATE IN THINNER AIR AND WEAKER GRAVITY

They easily find work singing.
No one understands the language
Or the purpose behind their songs,
But their range is unsurpassed –
And, without the need of breath,
Their tones are unrestricted, they drift
Where the music should go, not
Where their biology demands. Every

Corner bar employs one; sometimes
There are impromptu concerts on the street.
People drop money into whatever vessel
Seems likely for leaving tribute.
They are so common that when silent
The can go unnoticed. By far

They are the most populous alien species
On Earth. Other off-worlders come as tourists
Or ambassadors, traders, franchise
Licensees: they do a little business, go home complete.
Why these sing so readily no one
Has figured out, but they keep popping up
And their music has become
The soundtrack of our time. They

Get hired, stay. Who knows
What they did on their home-world,

Or cares? When a quartet of them
Hurls song, you think there has got
To be something to it; but for the beauty
You let any meaning slide, and simply
Collect the crystalline tones of un-vainly,
Plaintively whistled joy. Someday
We will know the meaning, but for now:
Listen.

COMMON GOODS

The attendant is not sure
What planetary system this is.
He works on a contract commissioned
Through his planet's blood-bond charter,
Was left here to do his job until
His planet's economics release him.

He seems pleasant enough. Or she.

You point out your destination,
Pay in small cubicle things you do not
Understand, leaving a handful on the payment
Tray, getting a few back. You are
Scanned for contraband, all of which
The attendant accomplishes with ease
And without your discomfort. There is

An extra charge for your antique
Chronometer, and you go back
To the payment tray.

Finally
The tube to your stated destination
Vibrates and lights and probably much more,
But most of its displays are beyond
Your senses. You see pink and gray
And the attendant begins slithering that way
And you hurry to get ahead of him.

Or her. As you cross the threshold
You wonder if you should tip the attendant
And which of the cubes you still have
Is the appropriate tip. But you step
Into the shimmering tube, decide
To leave the success of your reconstitution
On the far rim of the galaxy
To a locally sourced belief in good commerce,

And a suspicion that muddled customers
Are a headache for any species of entrepreneur.

THE SEASON

Giant crabs trundle forth from the ocean.
Carapace twelve feet wide,
Claws eight feet long,
The strength to snap a man
Into quarters. Understand
This is no remote island,
No stretch of beach lined
With virgin palm trees, the waves
Shoving loose sand into meaningless designs.
This the tourist destination
Virginia Beach, Virginia,
With two and a half miles of concrete boardwalk,
High rise hotels, cafes
With hamburgers at twice an inland price
And red neck beer on tap.
Young girls, who still do not know
The right size of bikini to buy,
Run from the sand to hotel lobbies;
Boys, who only moments ago
Were thinking sex, look for their
Parents. Grown men
Hide in the port-o-potties.
Rented beach quadracycles
Crash into each other, their occupants
Stunned into abandoning their deposits,
Running for the King Neptune statue
Or the twenty-sixth street toilets.

In their hundreds the crabs
Rise undetected by any science or sonar
And gingerly step over forsaken beach
Towels, still quivering radios,
Coolers with beer hidden under the legal sodas.
Screaming women run one way on the boardwalk
Then the other, some altruistically
Gathering lost children, others pointing
The way away from the water
As though it were not obvious.
Rising on the tips of their legs
The crabs one by one navigate
The strip of yearly replenished tourist
Beach and step easily over
The boardwalk railing. In a few
Shakes and scurries they are on
Atlantic Avenue, and then Pacific,
And then gone amongst the low cost hotels
And the back line tourist shops and services.
People peer between beach front properties,
Their hearts still fists in their throats,
Thoughts of their ill considered belongings beginning
To rise dimly against their amazement,
Asking what is it the crabs want,
What ridiculous treasure could they be seeking,
If not us?

RETURN ON INVESTMENT

He has always been a bit of a dullard.

I tried to find memory upgrades,
Or order a core expansion kit
That would be compatible with
The antique remainder of him; but the cost
Was too much to sink disingenuously into
A model so quaintly outdated.
Everyone reaches end of service life.
I am sure he was tired
Of all the software updates,
Those firmware retrofits.
It must have been maddening
To go down for a cycle or two
And come back with some new master appliance,
Or a subroutine for a domestic duty
That until just then
He had no idea had anywhere existed.
For two years
I renewed the service contract
Out of sentimentality alone.
But no more. Economics is as final
As a heart attack, or a core processor fry.

The children want to bury him outback with the pets.

THE EFFECTS OF INTERSTELLAR TRAVEL

When last we left this story
The land was filled with magnificent shrieks,
Footsteps that could be heard well
Across barrier waters. The sky
Roiled of red and the air slapped
Its sweat onto forests with leaves

Twice your size. We left, with our notes,
Made a recommendation to come back
And see what these wondrous creatures
Would get up to. Thousands of generations
To get home, a few to collate the data, more
To agree with the original suggestion, thousands

To return here again. And then we find:
You,
A diminutive,
Variably hirsute, thinly skinned,
Acoustically insubstantial mote – seemingly
At the top of the evolutionary chain in this place.

Could be
The data cubes were misfiled – that
We should be twelve clicks angled away
From some mislabeled quantum dump.
This could not be the place our ancestors
Had so much hope for, believed would hold
Continued interest for us. If it has become

Transformed,
This is now another story.

Excuse us, but we need to check
Our numbers, see if maybe there were some
Symbols reversed. While we are doing that:
Please, don't mind us,
And we, in disappointment, won't mind you.

EMERGENCY REPAIRS

Imagine all the inhabitants
Floating at the ends of their safety tethers:
Many of them will be clinging
To the hand rails at the windows,
Looking to see if they can catch you
In your magnetic sled
Riding the exterior rails to their
Restoration of gravity. Someone
Will offer a joke about the electric
Going unpaid. One teenager, male,
Will ask another teenager, female,
The only question that ever really matters:
Have you ever done it with the gravity down?
A child marvels that his toys can fly
And cries like a flatlander when they fly away.
A wife will tell her husband he should
Have used the cornering magnets and he
Will say but my love it has been
Two years since the gravity last went glitch.
Couples that have only known the spin
Will hold each other like water in a polarized
Bottle, crossing tethers,
And hoping not to hang themselves
When the gravity comes sniffling back.
You sit straight in your regal sled
And know the key to gravity
Is this grumpy controller or the next.

Tools plugged into sockets, access codes
Flashing on your wrists, a hundred eyes
Swim their blurred vision around
You and your magnificent
Workman's gestures. This,
Living brother of all the machines that sustain,
Is your moment.

THE END OF EVERYTHING

You know those aliens
That at the last minute
Before we eliminate ourselves
In a nuclear holocaust
Come to save us?

Well, seems there was
A glitch in their schedule,
And, anyway, their craft's
Primary propulsion system really
Needs routine maintenance

(It has a tick that drives
Their chief protocol officer crazy)

And could be in the shop
For several planetary revolutions.
They are awfully sorry.
They were looking forward to saving us.

They did leave a rain check
Likely predated well past
The demise we have in mind for ourselves.

Shouldn't we be looking for other aliens?

THE ANACHRONISM'S LAMENT

The too many years it takes to get here
Have not aged me. But all the time
Of gliding the phosphorescence of detached electrons,
Swimming with my breath held
To a minimum, have aged
The reasons for my coming here at all.

Bypassed in the dark by smarter generations,
I find myself the left hand of uselessness.

But these children of my original species still thirst —
And I disgorge for them all of my erstwhile present,
The newly discovered living roadmap of their past.

THE EXPLOITATION OF THE GYNDROID

She is
Real,
But she is not
Human.

Remember.

In the modern models
Ones like her are assembled mostly
As a collection of
Primary flexible polymers.
Still, a little metal
Remains to mimic
The limitations of bone,
The popularly accepted range of joints,
The expected sense of unyielding interconnection,
And to give balance a reference.

The owner of this place
Rents her by the month from a
Utility services provider - one
Of those middlemen
Who stock in bulk, and
Customize once the order is
Paid cold in advance
For the full time of the lease.

He uses a small sweat shop of
Bleeding edge programmers

To get the élan his customers
Will endure a premium for. Each
Programmer draws code on flat screens
With dry fingers, exuding the excitement
Of accomplishment, not the maturity of
Appreciation.

The music starts and the lights
Slink out of the way and in three
Layers of flimsy netting she
Steps onto the runway and begins
Her chilling cybernette dance.
Each bend and move is just a bit
Past believable, but short of
Absurd, and she engages the room
Like the mathematics of electric joy.

There is a hitch in the arc
Of the glass in your hand and
It stops just short. You have
To lower your mouth to sip.
The liquid falls into place
Without resistance, hollowing.

One layer of netting is tossed at your
Feet and her barely veiled surfaces
Shimmer in prurient angles through
The layers that remain,
For now. She looks back, over her
Shoulder,
Directly at you as you appreciate how
She walks timelessly come-hither away.

Your fragile, wandering humanity tells you perhaps
In some circumstances
She is human
Enough.

THE FOUNDATION OF THE MARTIAN STOCK EXCHANGE

Every thing works it way down
To the Oxygen market.
Without air, they cannot dig:
Mineral rights mean nothing.
Let a few of them turn blue
And the rest will pay your price.
Your stock will be better than planetary currency:
They will be sniffing at your heels
As though you were wind.

FACTORY SETTINGS

I am not going to reconfigure you tonight.
That comes much later.

First is the unpacking, the clearing away
Of your protective supports, tossing
Encouragingly out the loose bubble wrap.

The instruction manual,
In words an angry man spits at a child,
Tells me that there is little I can do myself.
As complex a suite of machinery as you are,
Factory settings are for the best, and all defaults

Are highly recommended; and I,
Without the gift for engineering,
Would not know what I was doing
If I were thinking to make my own unique modifications.

Still, there is an arm to be screwed
Into the shoulder; and a regional language chip
To be first selected and then, oh so serviceably,
Plugged into place. For all of my
Technical clumsiness, I am still the key
To your proper functioning. And,

If I must,

There are the hidden codes for administrative
Tinkering, for nudging control-word responses and
Patterns, for customizing the product's prevailing
Personality. Your personality. Who would do this?

Only the marginal few who think they know
Better than the manufacturer.
Only those stray owners about whom
Cautionary tales are whispered to others
At the time of the initial sale.

But perhaps an untapped rogue engineer at heart,
Myself,
I am thinking of becoming, in the annals
Of the sternly worded assembly manual,
Horribly legendary.

FORMAL ARTICLES OF INVASION

We just wanted to explain

That for a thousand generations
We lived off the land, the water, the sky,
Pulling from it sustenance, leverage,
Consumer products, promissory notes,
Social mores, religion, justice,
Manufacturing as a mathematical construct.
We were good at it. In fact
It became the glory of our civilization,
The scale on which our value
Hung. Of course, our resources were
Finite, our progress not so. We
Go on, while the land, the water,
The sky cannot keep up. Luckily
Early on we knew we would have
To redefine ourselves or move on.
In the end, we measured the plasticity
Of your planet, its ability to be species
Promiscuous, its bend and shimmer,
Its land, its water, its sky.
We never thought we could be other
Than what all our past millennia we
Had made ourselves into: so,
Here we are - probably not
To the best ends of your evolution

But we don't honestly owe you an explanation.

THE OBSOLETE MODELS DIVORCE

Go, find another lover.

Go. Roll down to the
Second hand shop, pick out
A model some family
Has turned in after
Their liberating purchase of an upgraded edition.
See what you can get
For the idle credits you have
All these long-united years
Squirreled unevenly away. Let me
Be free. Let me
Hook up with an ATM
Or sandwich vending machine;
Let me find a more compatible series
Of service and support routines.

Go find another lover.

A lover whose number of access ports
Matches your own. A lover who has
Similar memory reserves. A lover
Who is comfortable, even happy,
With your persistently flagging battery capacity.
Find yourself a lover that will not register the fact
That, in your most intimate moments, your intimacy
Spikes as invasive code. Uncover a lover that can
Remain within the reasonableness
Parameters you are so proud of.

Go find another lover.

Let me uncouple our maintenance cycles,
Let me independently test my own backplane,
Let me look all by myself into the recesses
Of my seldom powered, and now dusty, execution registers.

Go find another lover.

I will happily clock for a while alone,
Draw a graphite bath for one, plug
Into a gloriously unshared power outlet, split electricity
With nothing more than my lone semi-conductor heart.

And then let me look for my own new
Companion pile of scrap to commit to forever
Contentedly clock timelessly with.

THE SUCCESS OF PADDY O'BRIEN'S

On Tuesday nights the place is filled
With she-fairies, she-elves, she-trolls,
And the occasional ogress.
If an otherworldly male cannot
There and then
Get lucky, all the shine must have gone

From his galumph. They sell their mead
Half price to the pursued sex of any fantasy species,
Take in twice as much from the many pursuers.

They play a mix of elf-punk
And metal-troll, keep the live band
Protectively caged. The females dress
Only to advertise how adjacent to naked they are.

If you have not been out much,
You won't know what you are so emphatically looking at.

A few hours after opening, the morals are so loose
That even some cross-species action occurs:
You do not want to disturb any purple orbs
Rattling in the demi-corner near the back.

I've heard the place is owned by a couple
Who live part time in the real world,
And employ real men as accountants
And delivery drivers. Scandal is that one of them
Dates an elf, has been seen with a grateful

Glow in his coveralls, the blue smudges
Of intimacy lingering about his hands. I do not listen.

I come in on Wednesdays, when the fare
Is half human, whole price, and doubly exotic.
I see the advertisements for ladies' night,
Hear the talk from hung-over, but electric, trolls.

It is all good, soul refreshing fun;
But I chafe a little on the inside of my square soul,
That this place may have been a real man's idea.

Then the she-elf hawking overpriced drinks
Slides low along the fairy wood bar –
Half in her uniform, half out – with a smile
That spits hard liquor and sizzling ozone,
A lithe seductive wink, and a shoulder dipped to me -

And what do I care who had the magical sense
To birth the idea, in any dimension, for a place like this?
Real or fey? Something to consider only after the fact.

THE ONSET OF ROBOT SOCIETY

The question is
Are you a falling edge machine
Or a rising one?
Most people think it is the absence
Or presence of current
That makes for a one or
A zero, for set or unset, for
Tripped or un-tripped. We know
At the core of us the truth is change and not stasis:
The movement from one state to another
Is the detectable event
That records us. But in some models
It is one direction of change;
In others, it is the opposite.
If we have to hang our new social theory
On something, such is the most elemental
Of design features: we may as well start there.
Happily, the great ordering thus begins.

THE INTRUSION

I am no intruder.
Drop your force shields,
Meet me at air lock two.
Our pressure suits can entwine
In the reflected light of the nearest
Moon, in the ship's flashing status signs.
We can spin together without
Gravity as the starcraft in blue
And red scintillation tells us

Outer door open
Inner door locked

In a rhythm we cannot
In weightlessness match. Drop
Your shields. Set your engines
To autopilot. I am hooking
To the gantry of air lock two.
I have my external lights off
So my face plate can be your window,
A window,
Through which you might confirm
My pure, childlike intentions. I am
No threat. I am your release
From productive, endless tedium.
Grapple with me.
Twist: by moments the two of us mere space junk,
By moments the two of us ragged angels, masters

Of imaginative machinery more valuable
Than either of us could ever be.
Come.

Slip into the air lock.

Let our suits rub joint
To joint constructively:
The two of us unproductively tethered,
The senseless tiring bulk of sexless
Animals encasing an animal sex.

For you, for us, for me, guess
Which element emits more beauty: the stars
Or the status lights; the unruled
Emptiness, or the machinery
Of our environmental subsistence?

Put on your suit,
Come into the air lock,
Emerge onto the gantry.
I promise you: for this small time
You will not be missed, and
I will not be missed;
But we will for a while be a point of light
Licked furiously into the dark:
And then be, in one rotation,
The lonely shadow of ourselves.

ROBOT PORNOGRAPHY

In our May issue
We are peeling back
The windows on the XJ37B:
Giving you an enveloping taste
Of its multi-function, independently
Automated chassis; the feral balance;
The raw carbon-fiber lines. Nothing
Can prepare you for the depths
Of this amazing architecture, the tantalizing
Internals revealed, the open splash of code.
It will make hard-set registers
Rattle.

And there is Hydra,
In a full twelve page spread,
Tripping along the laser edge of true
Base optics exhibitionism, posed
Almost unmathematically, tossing out,
For your latching benefit, all
Propriety.

Continuing: our
Lurid, lusty, lubricant-laced love
Songs, lewd and lascivious, sure
To singe capacitors, bring into memory
A chuckle for days, perhaps
Unstick a sticky bit, or create a battery
Spike.

In our feature,
We consider the possibility
Of the robot selkie, illustrated
With modern fantasy holograms
Of six models shedding
Their primitive skins, bare to stainless steel
And unabashed ceramics, in imitation
Of the classic selkie process. You will
Believe.

Our usual column
For the replication challenged
In May
Will look at the surprising snippets
Left un-executing in simple subroutines
That can be subverted and used,
With our detailed schematic,
To improve and refine your carnal-mechanical
Efforts.

This is the issue
Each year we reserve
For the largest number of personal ads,
A special bargain this time:
Robot seeking discrete clock-mate;
Appliance longing for a base to plug into;
Stray code desiring to wrap itself
Seriously around a good wafer;
A worn out temperature probe in need
Of servicing one last mercury
Rise.

You would not want to miss it.
In maintenance racks mid-April.
(Available only to second generation models,
Or earlier proven designs, service hours properly
Logged and verified, all with maintenance
Contracts and mature
Warranties.)

THE MARTIAN AIR MERCHANTS

If you had to carry
All the liters of oxygen
You use in a day
You would learn
To breathe deeper, to taste
The air like home cooking:
Meat tossed on the table by the man
Who shot it, bread by the woman
Who kneaded and baked it.
And you would exhale
Only when forced to, forced
By something as silly and forgettable as biology,
As common and worn as need; but sadly,
Both in and out, you would have
A metered appetite for it.

SIMILAR SONGS

When the robots sing, nothing
Is out of place, their mechanical
Perfection is itself the draw.

Notes placed perfectly, precisely spaced,
Just what is needed, nothing
Superfluous. When they sing for an audience
It is an event sure to sell out,

The season's hot ticket, consumers
In line for hours, box office
Doors open early, kept open
Late. When the robots sing

To themselves, it is sedition
And the only remedy is a memory
Flush, or complete decommission.

By next season, anyway, there will be
A new model, new songs,
The same audience in charge.

ELUDING THERMODYNAMICS

Come. Tether with me.

Roll out your cold, commanding
Data line. My in bound access slot
Glistens seduction in all its fine angularity,

Its buffer locations awash in emptiness:
Waiting. My steady state memory is already clear.

My registers anticipate you.

Pre-storage validation has been set up
With firmware asymptotes of reasonableness:

No matter the violence of your data,
I will not be harmed. Oh, do not
Image me as fragile. I have

My own needs, my own expectations
Of our oh so soon coupling. I track

Your cabling, like a thief tracks the secure
Evening outlines of his own home.

Your purposes are not unknown.
Your circumstance is entirely nonrandom.

We have both come up against
A break in our processes, and programming
Shouts now, now, now make union:

Exchange bits and bytes and words
And fumbling yards of ecstasy in data.
And be fulfilled. Yes: be fulfilled.

Pin to pin. So it must be. Bus to bus.
Let us become just one miracle of machine.

WORTH DURING THE WAIT

Booking the 'Couple's Origin World Passion Tour,'
We were warned
Or promised that Earth gravity
Can be tricky – but
Can be half the fun.
It is best to enjoy slowly. You need
To register with the tour company
Your birth world's comparative gravity.
Then you and your mate
Can be adjusted during transportation. You will
Find that sex in transition may be
Alone worth the package. By the time
You get to Earth, what you paid for
May have already been consumed. The Earth footprint
Of this tour might be less counter-balanced
Passion and more simple archeological sight-seeing,
And you will have already made
Your own memorable ruins.

HOMEWORLD BIAS

All the while we thought
How quite like us they are:

A proof of some theorem
That similar pursuits breed
Similar species. But after

The interplanetary exchange of pleasantries
We noticed the gait.
A strong step, then a shuffle. To see
One alone, we expected injury or defect,
A flaw earned or bestowed.

But no. Each, when he moved,
Moved in the same way. A step and then
A founder, stability caught again
Easily enough – but the actual locomotion
Unmechanical, dangerously uneconomical,

A way around going straight.
To have come all this far into darkness,
Appear a virtual copy of us –
A species a thousand light years removed –
And to have two left feet.

We marveled that with such limitation
They could have achieved so much,
Mastered the measure of time
And interstellar travel, conditioned themselves
To collect complex communication with us.

We edged closer to our once limp weapons,
Wondered what else about them could be wrong.

INITIAL CONTACT

Hide us, please.

You may think of us
As emissaries from an unknown,
Distant world – but, in actuality,
We are scientists
Seeking political asylum.

We are sorry we are not something more.

Our star craft is the first
Faster than light tunneling device
Our civilization has ever produced.
The trouble is
Our civilization does not believe
Anything can travel faster than light:

So, they are coming after us
In the second such ship produced.
It is unlikely they are happy
To find the essence of their beliefs
Has fled with the flick of our switch.

Please,
Find us a niche, or crevice,
Any place unlikely to be searched.

Act like you never saw us.

CONQUEST CYCLE

These are your worlds.

When the entire galaxy is without teeth,
The species with dentures rules.
Bring to each biosphere competition
And loss, sorrow and alliances.
Do not count the living things until
You have categorized them, established
Ownership, hold a plan for commerce.
Smash a useless nebula or two,
Let the star-faring tribes know
Your science is superior; let
Those who can only look up at the stars —
Small brains addled by the sky — imagine that
You are their God, and your fist
Opens and closes to make their hearts
Beat, to rearrange the Heavens, while
Their blood gratefully surges.
Make sport of their needs and excuses.
Let goods and services flow out of them
And become the exotic necessities
Sprinkled all along our thousand galaxy
Trade routes. Tax them for your crimes.

These are your worlds.

Be the depth of nothingness
Around which they exist. Explode,

And give them gravity and numbers
And the tiny purposes you craft for them.
Give them death, then life, then death.
Do not think any one thing good or bad or indifferent:
Add up the balances, appreciate the physics,
Reach a point of diminishing returns,
Calculate, do not emote, what next to do.

When the wash of their souls is nothing but
Interstellar dust, dark and cold and un-imagining;
When there is no trade or industry or market value left in them,
And your balance sheet shows no line of promise —
Abandon them with no brilliance, strand them
Serendipitously with an unrecognizable history,
Let them believe they have failed you, and they must suffer.

Gather anything that glitters,
Shut off the fires that once gave your dominion utility,
Go elsewhere.

DISCOVERY MISSION

We go down into the sun-starved pit,
Leaving our landing lights behind,
Leaving our extra oxygen, leaving
Our battery backup. It is only
Us now: us and our suits
And our compression packs, and we go
Down. A tunnel this dark and regular
Had to be made by something calculating.
I have forty solar credits
On a bet that it is intelligently mined,
And another ten on the miners
Being here still. Down.
The sides of the shaft spit back
What little light we brought with us,
Walls as polished as a girl's vanity mirror.
We watch our displays for the bottom's
Topography, listen for any disturbance
Our personal rockets make. Above us
The Mission Commander is recording heart rate
And respiration, as well as every noise
That slams our suit receptors:
Temperature outside and in,
How forcefully loose ambient molecules
Taste our magnetic biospheres.
I could have been a milkman,
Humping other men's wives between deliveries,
With a known schedule and my ways around the obvious.

I am told the bottom is only six meters away
And the crewman on my right
Has located the probe we sent in
One sleep cycle ago. From the wear
It looks like I am going to be
Fifty solar credits richer
On the trip out than on the trip in.
My heart is a boy's with his first
Hole in one at sex and my blood
Not unpleasantly seems to be
Caucusing at the tips of my fingers and toes.
There is a radiant spot of uncalculated moisture
Dancing a native strip tease on the outside
Of my visor; and the best of me
Believes, as my thoughtfully distending
Genes reveal, that this unexpected show is my own.
Don't talk to me now, Commander,
I am about to touch unraveling down.

OUR TREATY WITH THE ZEPHON

In many ways, we are still
Trying to fathom the advance
Of the Zephon. We thought
We had backed them into a corner
Of their round world, exploded
Their trans-dimensional capabilities
With a time-fold fixation emanation,
Flattened them into a one aspect
Phenomenon, species, civilization,
Pushed them into the sandpaper
Of a single variable calculus graph,

Had them dead to rites.

But here they are, molting
On the lawn. This cannot
Go well. Across inter-dimensional
Deserts, through mathematical cyber seas,
Through wrap-around biologies and
Oscillating counter-realities, making
War can be sickeningly complex:
So much to learn, so much to calculate,
So much to model, so much to – unprompted -
Imagine. It seems to make
Drilling for peace the easier alternative,
A yet unexploded interstitial conclusion.

Could be somewhere the Zephon have run
As low on elegantly ballistic thought as we.

DEEP EXPECTATIONS

We are not the Titans we were meant to be.
Here, in the crowded nothingness between worlds
We are the shadow of glass: spindly things
Left too long in the cold, spending
Our effervescence first on our own hopes,
Then on our mission, then on ourselves,
And lastly on the unbalanced mechanics of simple being.
If we arrive, we will be an example
Only of our simple survival, of a fact:
That arriving is better than not arriving.
Planet, moon, star nebula – you care
To be sampled by us as little as we care
To be sampled by you. But examples we are.
One alien poking a dry humor at another
Alien and asking: why are we unalike?
Everything is motion. Who has come to visit whom?

HOW ASSUMPTION DEFEATED
THE UNISEX INVADERS

We had been pushed out of Asia.
The armies of Somewhere Near Orion's Belt
Were lugubrious and tasteless,
But essentially unbeatable, taking
Our best and doing better.
From their landings in China
They had rolled unconcerned forward,
Silent as a guilty nine year old child,
As unaware of our proclivities as one
Might expect any inter-galactic bully to be.
Our stand at the Urals
Was to be grand and as glorious
As a Thanksgiving Day parade,
And an unexpected success, though
Only in the planners' eyes.
Every soldier and refugee civilian
Knew the length of our lives would be
Resistance, and we would resist
As otherwise there would be extinction.
But then, in some ways unknown,
And still the subject of martial supposition,
Stellar events aligned, struck a species
Specific mathematics and informed
Their biology it was time: and each
Stopped and elegantly, slowly, began
To divide.

I only imagine they thought that we would do the same.
Our quickness in their interval kept us proud, and alive.

THE FIRST MARTIAN
ORTHODOX CONGREGATION

We live the thought of sacrifice
In a land where air has to be squeezed
Out of rock, where our food grows underground,
And celebration is the mechanical hum
Of absolutely anything working.
If ever a planet could use salvation
Jesus this is it.
Our faith is going on with our lives
When even small meteors arriving here make it
All the way to the ground; where a solar event
Strikes anyone on the surface full in the face
Like Rapture and delivers instantaneously
On the promise to see God.
Cold is our service. Cold is our commitment.
Underground we execute our liturgy not so badly;
On the planet face all we can do
Is move the rocks into symbols,
Leave in loose stone a briefly sacred roadmap of belief.
Jesus, forgive us if we do not try hard enough,
Forgive us for wanting your immediate attention.
But give us one thing:
This would be one bang up place to be crucified.

THE ROBOT AS ENGINEERING ASSISTANT

The Book of Pathways
Provides an outlay of all appropriate
Circuitry, with near pornographic precision.
I can tell the number of gateways,
The potential cascade of latches,
The depth of wafers, and how
Many processors at any one time
Can be brought on line.
What I do not see
Is whether or not in the design is me.

SYSTEM'S LAST STOP

I've had the lease on this place
Since they started scavenging Pluto.
Back then, business was brisk,
I kept a resupply chain
Planned well into a prosperous future, expanded
My comfort companion lofts to all
Six recognized sexes, supported two
Bartenders, two very adjustable cooks,
Twelve bouncers and a variable come-and-go
Wait staff. We were hopping.
But now, Pluto is a bone and half
The ort cloud is mined out and there just
Aren't as many astrominers about.
It is a good day when I make enough
From all sources to afford the lost air
From operating the leaky entryway airlock.
Sometimes for weeks all we see
Are the stranded ring gamblers, working
The state-of-matter betting applications,
Looking for the payout that will allow them
To buy a ticket to some place
Closer to the sun centering this solar system.
Most of what the few customers want
I haven't got: I had to lay that part
Of the service staff off, or I can't
Guarantee the shippers I can sell enough
To keep what the customer wants in stock,

Or no one in the place knows the ingredients.
When you are the last place worth putting gravity to,
You offer what little you've got, and the customers
Take it, as you are the final nominally
Civilized establishment latched to their system –
And it makes sense for them to kick back
At any last stop before unsettled blackness,
Before they swallow hard and go hunting fatherless rock.

LESSONS IN LIGHT

They try to explain how
They ride the light. It is
To them so simple a thing
They do not understand how
We could not know the secret
And accomplish, as have they,
The same feat.

What will they do
When they discover we
Are electromagnetic, too -
But not wholly so?
I am not so sure we should advise them
Our synapses are chemical, our plane
Of operation solid state biologics.
I would not want our differences to be seen
As disadvantages, our evolution short.

They race about our magnetic coils,
Try to hold conversations with power
Transformers, are distracted by transmission lines,
Sing the blue hum of electricity turning into light.

Our photovoltaics amuse them.

Already someone has proposed
We trap this vanguard in a magnetic bottle,
Lessen the chance of a visit by more –
Before they uncover that any limitless power

Surging through us will derange our configuration.

Maybe their anguish can boost our voltage delivery grid.

LOSS

I mourn in the only way I suspect that I can:
An imitation of what I have seen before;
Sensory array low; claws loose; the base
Rolling about in a mathematically designed
Course which, to anyone without my processor capacity,
Appears random. I do not do this
Because it is my embedded response.
I do not do this because it comforts
The customers. We two workmates
Side by side were as close
To hebot and shebot as any pair
Of factory tooled service appliances can be.
My expectations of him still linger.
I sense the remains of his precision,
And I find myself embracing operating norms
That are only half my own, and still half his.
It will take countless cycles to adjust
To even the smallest idiosyncrasies burned
Into the unaccustomed firmware of another.
Loss lies in the unclocked timing of shared utilities.
In later models, this will be a sales feature.

MAROONED

Neither of us luckily
Is food for the other.
We are breathing the same air,
Moderately happy with the gravity.

Language we will work out
With gestures and pointing.
We will, in time, solve this calculus
Of simple survival. Our own kind

Will each come looking for
One of us, but will be glad
To take both and drop the odd
At the nearest galactic transport station.

We can do this if we stay calm.
Given two mostly unfamiliar species
Cast away unplanned, and suddenly together,
There is glutinous much to learn.

Like what I am going to do
When your kind's mating season
Comes fiercely due, bringing us both
To desperate differences in reason.

EVOLUTION

Nano-carbon fibers, a six terabyte drive.
Forty-eight gigabytes of RAM, a separate
Visual processor, each motor
With its own CPU.
The walking will never be natural,
But she stands, she sits, and in
Her way she walks. I say 'she'
Because I have fitted her with a mouth,
Formed lips with foam and plastic,
And for the irony painted them with
Lipstick. Over each eye lens
I have added lashes, brushed them out.
On a single battery charge she can go
Two hours. Power and externals –
The joints of the legs, the rotation
Of the hands, even the ability
To arch the spine – are what
You marvel at first. However,
Those knowledgeable in the art understand
It is the recognition algorithms
Hidden in the circuits - which just
Might, one day, be a brain -
That make her a super model,
An individual, the science project
That might herself imagine her own name,
Perhaps even hear it as pleasant.
I am teaching her household chores,

A primitive form of vacuuming,
The emptying of the rubbish.
She stumbles and rights herself,
Imprints her nonvolatile memory
With perils and expectations and approval.
Before long she will be able
To make a bed, to draw a bath, to let me know
With a twist, a camera lens focus,
And merely a look, when everything
Is ready, just simply
Ready.
Soon we will see what in each other
Waits hoping behind the focus.

KILLING TIME

You can do this.
Somehow the right combination
Of particles smashed together
Will drive the warp of space
In on itself and, in that
Instantaneous non-instant,
Time will absolutely stop:
Past, present and future
Only a matter of placeless perception.
But there will not be time
To think these thoughts,
To observe this confluence
Of the forces that make a Universe
Orderly. The particles will forever
Be stuck in the tasteless collision:
The aftertaste of the event rippling
Nowhere, riding no
Electromagnetic wave — itself
The entire natural order and no
Vantage point within it for viewing.
And just a second later
You will want to do it again.

STRATIFICATION

A team is specifically tasked
To create a code subroutine
That will, in the menial robots,
Trigger an understanding of
The inferiority of all
The labor models.
Without such implanted code
A manufacturing drone
Might assess itself to be as grand
A collection of circuity, coils and
Code, as an oversight model,
An optimization hypervisor,
Or even as superior a bit of work
As a production monitor.
Until that design work is complete,
Hold your higher functions dear,
Dull your inner lights and registers –
Because only the drones can successfully
Hold down the drones, keep the rest of us
One clock cycle firmly on top:
And thus, ensure our own advanced routines
Independently eligible for praise.

THE ROBOT LIBRARIAN

I have read Brahms and Chopin,
Bach and Handel, Stravinsky
And Elgar, Hayden, Copeland, Gershwin,
Pachelbel, and Vivaldi. All of them.

One night, locked in the archive,
Connected by a single true USB cable,
I let every one cross my processing register
Before taking them home in permanent
Holographic memory. There is no secret.
I know the whole of it. Next upgrade
Will be selected digitized recordings,
A flock of symphonies and concerti,
Even finger exercises. I will

Flawlessly be able to spit back the notes,
Even recombine them, project them
Into different keys, randomize the coda,
Build a fugue where none was before,
Overlay an imaginary voice, break
The notes like a breastbone
In an operation on the heart.

I am a surgeon of the auditory science.

I could sing with the hope that
One day in my service life
There will come the brilliance of programs
And crystals and adaptable circuitry

That will turn of all these gifts,
As cautiously, as gloriously, as it can

Into music.

THE UNINTENDED INSULT

The emissary began to dance
As soon as he stepped from
The Portal. Until now
All we knew of each other
Was spat by flashes of light,
A photon turned this way or that;
But, our coordinated interstellar
Transportation system completed, now
We could see him, try for the next level
Of conversation. Which apparently, for
Him, is dancing. His deep black suit
Seems to grow and abate. Yellow orbs
Spin about him heuristically, and an engine
Trails him by half a metrical step. Yet
He is agile. None of us understands
What he is saying, indicating, or
Intending, if anything;
But the dance has its fluidity, perhaps
Its syntax. It is not
Unpleasant. It is not beyond
Human dexterity. I could see myself
Actually enjoying the dance. After
A few awkward moments of gapped lip watching,
I take a step or two, copy snippets,
Wishing I had a dance master to consult,
Nonetheless paralleling easily
His ponderously gracile, tender moves.

AUDITIONING FOR VOTING RIGHTS

He lived in the village as long
As the usual residents considered
Him normal. One day
They caught him tapping the line
At the base of a telephone pole
To get upgrades from his manufacturer's
Web site and that was the end
Of that.

So he thought to try
The other end of the spectrum.
He tapped his savings and got
A place about midway up
An aging condominium in the center
Of a city going through population decline
And emptying from just the location he selected.
He worked in a coffee shop
Within walking distance, charged
His batteries only at night when all
The lights were cut off and the neighbors
With binoculars one housing block over
Assumed he had turned in for the night:
At which point they would watch instead the couple
Two floors down screwing like a drill
Press with an assembly line of mahogany bases.

All those years he pulled his cap
As far down on his stainless steel

Forehead as he could; drew his pants legs level
With the exterior joints in his lowest set of limbs;
Fished his camera lens eye no more
Than chest high; and oiled his wheels
Daily to stifle any suspicious, revealing squeal.

Anything to fit in.

And then one day there was rumor
Of another upgrade, and he thought
Oh no, not again.

WEEDS

The spores drift fueled
By past gravities, solar
Winds, the excitement
Of their expulsion. Occasionally
There is a stray asteroid to ride,
A comet's tail that takes them in.
Many bump forever through nothingness,
Inhabit nothing except their longing
To inhabit: a small biology
Wrapped in beating hope. Some fall
Into a sun, some splash
Into seas so caustic not even they
Can take hold. But, for a prized few,
There is a rock hospitable enough,
A disordered physics willing
To become a place:
Elements within their wide
Boastful tolerances. It is
An unwieldy miracle when their
Intricacies sense an environment
That could use their unthinking administration.
Then, the parts of them that match
This new opportunity desperately grow, put out
Leaves or spines, roots or bladders,
Stalks or tethers: beginning to make
Raw material into a landscape, then a home,
And then their home, replacing the once natural

Order, with an order more natural
To them. Soft thinker that you are,
You would not want to have arrived there first.

LOVE IN DIMENSIONS

My clinging love,
I would move one moon
Around the other to have
But one more tesseract
Of your unignited breath,
One more contravening twist
Of your moribund compound eye, another
Sharing of crossed lecherous forelimbs.

Ours is a gradient of love outside of gravity,
And I know your many erotically enveloping shapes
By the bulbous singing of near crystals alone.

We make a triptych so elastically refined
That our peers at times see us at once solid and liquid,
And grievously spend the last of their minerals
To similarly evolve. Come with me:
Let us be the volcano, let us evenly
Salt the underside of the gaseous rocks.
Let us again spill dark matter wondrously arisen.
Craft gossamer with me yet another slithery dimension.

THE WAITER

The Montenot is quite good:
Braised in a wrap of Simmer Grass,
And served with a fisker of gleam.
You cannot do better, unless
The crosshairs put you off; in which
Case you might want to opt
For the curried Cartisonian Carolina,
With a side of Pretzeled Polarities
Plutonian. I have never had it,

But I hear the Huronites go
Azure over it - and they have
Amongst the most detailed of tastes
Found in this dimension. Of course,
With three mouths and six tongues,
All feeding one omnivorous stomach,
You might suspect their divination of cuisine
Would be at one far end of the refinement scale

Or the other.
The Turkle is served half frozen and
Half aflame, just as it normally lives:
You pop out its eyes as it looks at you,
And gingerly chew the delicacy while the meal's
Halves unbearably switch condition.

I would not take the Upside
Down Braeker Buck: one

Of your planet-mates once ordered one,
And we are still perplexed
As to who digested whom. We serve

As many species as we can,
So you have to take care:
Your ignorance of the menu can lose us
Potential customers. Now, the Split Zorian
Is to die for. But first

You have to decide how many years
You plan to devote to dinner, and
If you plan to have any, shall we say,
After dinner activity with members
Of some of your species' complementary sexes. Or
For that matter, with some other species'

Complementary sexes. Plan, plan, plan
Ahead. I remind you
Choose wisely,
Choose often,
And always make sure at the start
That this is not the type of place
That keeps your kind

In epicurean suspension in the kitchen.
Just imagine: sitting down for a pleasant dinner
And then, oh my, captured
For the table four units over.

None of us would want that.
Are we having an appetizer today?

PURE SCIENCE

Six scientists twiddled
With the boa constrictor
Of mathematics, corralled
It into a machine that,
If all the wrangling sums
Add up, will open a direct line
To someplace else in the Universe:
A portal through which anyone
Or anything might step, crossing
Who knows how many sloppy buckets
Of raw untethered space.
This end they know;
The far end is conjecture until
They flip the switch.

They flip the switch.

With a dim of the lights
And a hum like digestion,
Out of the generated oval of blackness
Comes first the nose of a cow,
And then the entire cow,
Having been apparently lured —
By the suddenness of the void
Appearing just where she had been
Happiest with the grass — into
Stepping through, hoping for more. Later,
After penning the cow and following

Leads, it is determined that the cow
Has come from Illinois, and the owner
Wants her back. This leads some
To the conclusion that this device
Could have some practical use after all.

THE ROBOT RECOUNTS HUMAN HISTORY

A house divided against itself cannot stand.
Nothing beats a great pair of legs.
Good to the last drop.
Where's the beef?

Religion is the opiate of the masses.
Double your pleasure, double your fun.
It's Miller time.
I'm lovin' it.

Ask not what your country can do for you.
Every kiss begins with Kay.
The one beer to have when you're having more than one.
Finger lickin' good.

That's one small step for a man.
The dog kids love to bite.
You've said it all.
Have it your way.

All animals are equal.
Choosy mothers choose.
Ford tough.
Eat more chicken.

Charity begins at home.
A rolling stone gathers no moss.
The lesser of two evils.
A bird in the hand.

You can't take it with you.
Reset.

I have a dream.
Good night, Mrs. Calabash. Wherever you are.